WHEN COYOTE WALKED THE EARTH

Indian Tales of the Pacific Northwest

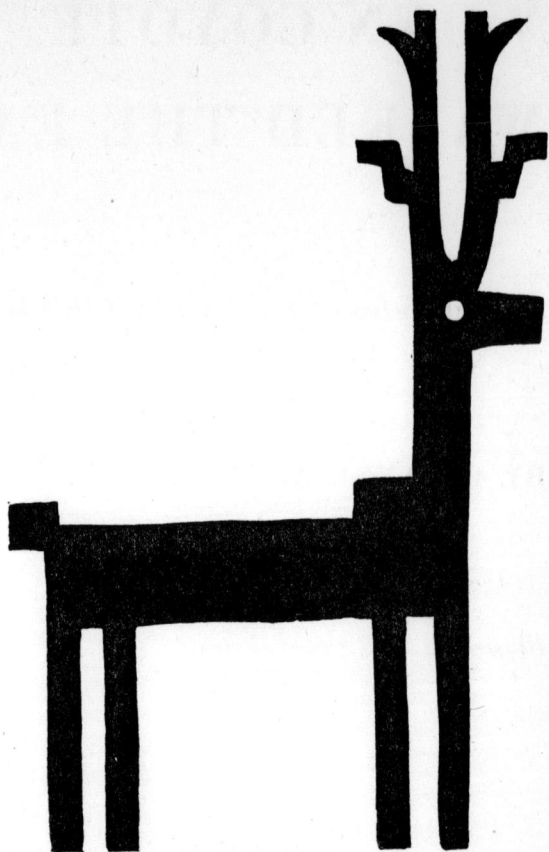

WHEN COYOTE WALKED THE EARTH

Indian Tales of the Pacific Northwest

BY CORINNE RUNNING

Illustrated by Richard Bennett

HENRY HOLT AND COMPANY · NEW YORK

Contents

C241694

WHEN COYOTE WALKED THE EARTH

Indian Tales of the Pacific Northwest

The Animals Determine
the Length of Day and Night

MANY and many years ago no one lived in the land but the animals. In those days the animals walked and talked like people. There were Grizzly, Fox, Wolf, Cougar, Beaver, Elk, Weasel, Coyote and many others. But Coyote was the strongest and most powerful of them all, and so he was chosen their leader.

Animals, of course, are not like that today. Before there were white people in the land—even before there were Indians—each of the animals, one by one, did something wrong and for their misdeeds they became the animals we know today.

1

In those early days, however, Coyote ruled all the animals. He was chosen by them to prepare the land for the Indians, for the animals knew that some day the Indians would be coming to live in the land, too. There were many things to be done first. It was Coyote who planned and did them all.

First he traveled through the land with a staff of wood in his hand, naming the mountains and the streams. He gave names to Mt. Rainier and Mt. Adams and Mt. St. Helens.

When he came to a big river he made a fish trap barrier by blockading the river. Then he made a dip net.

"You, fish! You, salmon! Enter the stream right here!" he said. "This will be a salmon river in the future and when the Indians come they will catch salmon here in dip nets."

He found other places in the river where the water boiled and bubbled. Fish came up on the surface of the water. Coyote said that in those places the Indians would spear salmon in the future.

He came to another river where there were falls. "How will the Indians catch salmon here?" he wondered. Then he wove a fish basket trap and tied it in position at the falls. After a while Chinook Salmon swam down the river and jumped into the trap. "That is the way the Indians will catch salmon in this river," Coyote said.

"Wren and Blue Jay and Pheasant will live near the falls and when the Indians come they will be their friends," said Coyote.

He walked on. "I shall go as far upstream as the salmon

2

go," he thought. "In the future there will be no salmon in the little brooks, but in the large rivers there will always be salmon."

Coyote spoke to the salmon. "Big Salmon," he said, "there is very fine country in the direction of the ocean."

The big salmon went out toward the ocean where they have remained ever since.

"Little fish!" Coyote called, "the country is fine up-river."

When he spoke, the little fishes broke away from the others and swam upstream. The big ones continued swimming downstream. And so it has been ever since.

Then Coyote came away from the river to a prairie. Here he placed roots, strawberries, and other food. "I will prepare food of all sorts so that when the Indians come to the land they will not be hungry. I will also make timber so that they may burn wood and keep themselves warm."

After Coyote had named the mountains and the streams, and put fish in the rivers and food on the land, there was still something to be done. For many years ago, when no one lived in the land but the animals, there was no day and there was no night.

Coyote said, "I will make the stars shine brightly at night so the Indians can see, and in the future Moon will travel at night, while his brother Sun will travel in the daytime."

All the animals began talking about this plan. They argued and argued, trying to decide how long the day should be and how long the night should be.

They finally agreed to hold a meeting and settle the question once and for all. Grizzly, Cougar, Wolf, Badger, and Coyote came early. But all the animals came because this was a very serious question and it had to be decided.

Bear spoke first. "There shall be five days and then there shall be one darkness. On the fifth day there shall be dawn."

Grizzly, the older brother of Bear, did not agree. "I don't think so, Bear," he said. "I think there should be darkness for ten years and then one dawn."

Rattlesnake spoke. "You are both wrong," he said. "Ten years is too long. I think five years of darkness would be better."

"Oh, no, Rattlesnake," said Bull Snake, Rattlesnake's younger brother, "I think three years is long enough for darkness."

They argued and argued among themselves. Finally Big Toad, who was there with a large number of his younger brothers, spoke.

"I think you're all wrong," he said. "You all want darkness for too long a time. The Indians will be here some day. They will not like darkness so long. I think there should be only one darkness and only one dawn."

"I think you're right, brother," said Frog, younger brother of Toad. "One darkness and one dawn."

At this Grizzly became very angry. He was a very powerful Being in the land and all the animals feared him. Rattlesnake, who was also powerful, was angry, too.

"No! No!" Grizzly and Rattlesnake shouted. "It shall not be that way!"

4

"Ten years," said Grizzly.

"Five years," said Rattlesnake.

No one agreed with either of them and they grew tired of shouting.

Then Grizzly suggested, "Let's have a contest. We'll argue it out. Whoever is strong enough to talk the longest will win."

All the animals started to argue. But one by one they became tired and dropped out of the contest. There was no one left but Grizzly and Frog.

"Ten years, one darkness," persisted Grizzly.

"One darkness, one dawn," answered Frog.

"Ten years of darkness," repeated Grizzly. "Ten years, ten years!"

"One darkness, one dawn!" said Frog.

All night they argued. Finally Grizzly was too tired to go on. Frog had the better of him and Grizzly gave up.

From that time until now there has been darkness for one night only. Nowadays, when you hear the frogs croaking at night they are probably telling the other animals how they won the argument with Grizzly.

How Spring Came

AFTER the animals had settled the question of how long day and night should be, a very cold winter came. Every stream in the land froze. Even the snow was frozen and lay hard and icy over the ground.

There was no food and the animals grew very hungry. The snow was so deep that they could not find food. Something had to be done.

Coyote called together all the animals who lived in the land. Bear, Grizzly, and all the blue jays were there.

"We'll sing," said Grizzly. "If we sing loud enough and long enough it may bring warm weather."

"Yes, we'll sing," Blue Jay said. "Maybe someone will sing who has the power to bring warm weather."

Bear and Coyote and Cougar and all the birds and animals sang. They sang loud and they sang long, but nothing happened. They became discouraged, but they did not give up. There must be others who could sing, too.

"How about the Water-Dwelling People?" asked Blue Jay.

That seemed like a good idea so they went to the Water-Dwelling People and asked them to sing. All the different fish under the ice in the streams sang. Black Bass and Trout led the chorus. But it was still cold and the land froze harder than ever.

Then the animals asked the roots and the berries and the fruits to sing. Wild Blackberry sang until his throat nearly burst. All the berries and the roots and the fruits sang. They sang loud and they sang long, but nothing happened. The ice on the river remained the same. The snow was unchanged and icicles hung on the trees.

Grizzly was just about to give up when he saw the five Dog brothers. They had been lying near the edge of the crowd and had not been paying much attention to what had been going on.

Grizzly walked over to them and said, "Why are you so unconcerned about this? Don't you know that it's a serious situation? You are going to sing, too!"

When Grizzly spoke all the animals obeyed.

"Very well," the oldest Dog brother replied, "but I don't think it will do any good. So many people have already been singing and they have accomplished nothing. But let us sing, brothers."

The five Dog brothers sang. After they had sung the

7

oldest brother said, "When we sing, our song echoes from the mountains. We'll go up on the mountain now and if our song follows us, then the weather will change. At dawn we'll be on top of the mountain, and if we have been successful, mist will settle along the mountain ridge. Then you will see deer coming down the side of the mountain." He turned to his brothers. "Come, brothers, let's sing as we go toward the mountain."

The five Dog brothers sang as they marched toward the mountain and started to climb.

The other animals waited patiently all night. Finally it was dawn. Suddenly they shouted happily. For there was mist on the mountain ridge. Quickly, suddenly, softer, warmer snow began to fall.

"The Dog brothers are bringing the deer!" Cougar shouted.

All the animals ran to the foot of the mountain and lay waiting.

"Look!" cried Coyote. "The snow is turning to water!"

"It's raining!" said Badger. "The snow is disappearing!"

"It's getting warm!" Grizzly said. "The Dog brothers have brought warm weather!"

Soon the deer came down the side of the mountain and there was plenty of meat for all the animals. It rained and all the snow and ice flowed away. The land became warm and spring came.

Sometimes in the winter you will hear an echo across a mountain valley and people call it the Weather Spirit of the Dogs.

8

The Origin of Fire

ONE DAY Coyote called all the animals together—Cougar, Grizzly, Beaver, Fox, Wolf, Rattlesnake, Frog, and all the birds. They gathered in a circle and when they were quiet, Coyote said, "I have called you together because there is another problem we must solve. We now have day and night and we now have spring, but we still have no fire. Soon the Indians will be here and they will want fire."

The animals had never thought of this before but they at once agreed with Coyote.

"How are we going to get fire, Coyote?" inquired Fox.

"First," explained Coyote, "we will all make arrows. Then we will shoot them up to the sky to make an arrow ladder so that we can climb up and take the fire from the Sky People."

After the animals had made their arrows, Coyote said he would shoot first. He shot an arrow but he did not hit the sky. It was close but not far enough.

Bear shot next, but he could not hit the sky either.

Elk shot but he, too, was unsuccessful.

All the large animals and birds tried, but none of them could hit the sky.

Then the small birds tried. Sapsucker was first. He may have been small but his arrow was the first to hit the sky. The other animals and birds cheered and clapped for him.

Wren stepped up. He measured the distance carefully and let his arrow fly. A cheer rose from the crowd. Wren's arrow had hit in the notch of Sapsucker's, the first arrow that had been shot. There were two lengths in the arrow ladder now. Every small bird tried and each shot an arrow into the notch of the one that had been shot before. The ladder was coming close to the earth.

"Let me try again," said Grizzly.

This time Grizzly's shot was successful.

"I'll try again, too," Bear said.

Bear's shot was successful and brought the ladder all the way down to the ground.

"Now we can start," said Grizzly.

He led the way and one by one all the animals and birds climbed up the arrow ladder to the sky. After they had all reached the top of the ladder they found themselves near a river.

10

"Now that we have reached the sky, how are we going to get the fire?" asked Grizzly.

"Let me float down the river to the Sky People's fish trap," Beaver suggested. "They will catch me there very soon and when they take me out of the river I can get the fire."

"A very good idea, Beaver," agreed Grizzly, "but it's dangerous. If the Sky People catch you they'll skin you."

"I'm not afraid," said Beaver. "Surely you know how long it will take the Sky People to skin me and you can be there in time to save me."

"Very true," nodded Fox.

"Please get there in time to save me!" Beaver said anxiously.

"We will," promised Grizzly. "You'd better go now, Beaver."

Beaver floated down the river into the Sky People's fish trap. Just as he had thought, the Sky People saw him right away.

"Oh, look!" they shouted. "A beaver is caught in our fish trap!"

"A beaver!" said one of the Sky People in surprise. "Why, he is from down below! How did a beaver from down below get up here?"

"Let's get him!" said another.

The Sky People ran to the river and took Beaver out of the fish trap.

"Let's skin him right away!" one of the Sky People suggested.

"Right away! Right away!" they all shouted.

Beaver was worried now. Would the other animals come in time to rescue him? But just as the Sky People were about to skin him, Timber Rabbit came with all the animals from down below following him.

When the Sky People saw all the animals from down below they were frightened and they dropped Beaver.

As soon as Beaver was free, he leaped into the burning wood and hid the fire under his fingernails. He took all the fire the Sky People had, and holding it under his fingernails, he ran to the arrow ladder. He and all the animals climbed down to earth again. When they were all safe on earth once more they broke the ladder.

Beaver took the fire from his fingernails and put it into the trees—as many trees as there were in the forest. When the Indians came to the land they were able to build fires, and since that time when a tree is chopped into logs, it is often burned.

Coyote Releases the Water Supply

IN the early days when Coyote ruled, the water supply of the land was held by the frogs. The frogs had dammed up all the water and it was held in one place where they stood guard over it at all times. The animals were forced to buy water from the frogs whenever they were thirsty and wanted a drink.

Coyote did not like this. He thought the water should be available and free to everyone. He decided to do something about it.

Coyote started out. He traveled to the place where the frogs stood guard over the water.

"I'm very thirsty," Coyote said to one of the frog women. "I've traveled a long way. May I have a drink of water?"

13

"Certainly," replied Frog Woman. "Anyone may have a drink of water who pays for it."

"But I have no money with me," Coyote answered.

"Then you can't have a drink," Frog Woman told him.

"All right," said Coyote, "I'll go home and get some money."

Coyote turned and walked into the nearby woods. There were camasses growing in the woods, and Coyote dug up a few of the plants. He cut off the stalks and rolled them into shapes that resembled money.

"This will fool the frogs," he said with satisfaction.

Coyote returned to the well where the frogs were still standing guard. He held out his hand and showed the frogs the camasses that looked like money.

"Now may I have a drink?" he asked.

"Yes, indeed!" answered Frog Woman, impressed with Coyote's money. "Help yourself."

Coyote kneeled down to drink.

"Don't drink too much water," Frog Woman warned him. "Five swallows is all you may have."

Coyote forced his hand into the earth. If he could get his hand far enough into the earth, he could tear it open and break the dam that was holding the water supply in one place.

Frog Woman saw what he was doing. She struck him very hard on the head.

"Help me!" she called to the other frogs. "Don't let him release the water in our dam!"

The frogs were angry. They struck Coyote again and again. But he kept his hand in the earth where the water

14

was dammed off. He worked quickly, scooping the dirt away to one side, making a channel through which the dammed-up water could escape. He bored through the earth and after a while it broke open, letting out the water in a great rush. Salmon and many other fish were freed as the dam burst open.

The frogs were helpless. Coyote's strength frightened them. They waited for him to speak.

"You will never keep the water back again," Coyote told them. "No one will have to buy water again. It will be free to everyone. In the future your home will be on the riverbank."

Bullfrogs have lived on riverbanks ever since.

The Animals Determine
Who Is To Be Elk

ONE DAY when Coyote was walking he found a pair of antlers. He decided to try the antlers on several animals to determine who was to become Elk. He called all of the animals together.

"I will try the antlers on your head," Coyote explained, "and whomever the antlers fit shall be known as Elk."

"I would like to be Elk," Jack Rabbit said. "Let me try them on."

Jack Rabbit put the antlers on his head. They fit very well.

"Very good!" said Coyote. "They seem to fit you very

16

well. Suppose you go away now and fatten yourself for three months."

Jack Rabbit went to the mountains for three months to eat and become fat. At the end of three months all the good hunters went after him. They pursued him for five days but when they finally caught him, they found that he was too lean.

"Let him go," said Coyote. "Jack Rabbit will never be Elk. The Indians will be coming to the land soon and the animal chosen to be Elk must be fat. We will try the antlers on someone else."

"Let me try them," said Timber Rabbit.

Coyote tried the antlers on Timber Rabbit's head.

"They fit!" cried the animals. "Let Timber Rabbit be Elk!"

"Go to the mountains for three months," Coyote told Timber Rabbit. "You will become fat in that time and then the animals will hunt you."

Timber Rabbit went to the mountains and three months passed.

"Timber Rabbit should be fat now," Coyote said. "We will hunt him."

The hunters gathered together. There were Cougar, Wild Cat, Wolf, Coyote, and all the other animals who liked to hunt.

They found Timber Rabbit. He ran and they pursued him. Over two mountains they pursued him. But when they caught him he, too, was found to be too lean.

"Let him go," said Coyote. "Timber Rabbit will never be Elk. We will have to find someone else."

It happened that nearby there lived two brothers, Sturgeon and his younger brother. They had heard about the search for Elk and were discussing it.

"Let's both go to the place where the animals are assembled," Sturgeon's brother said. "Perhaps the antlers will fit one of us. It would be a great honor to be chosen Elk."

Sturgeon did not want to go and he did not want his brother to leave him. He became very angry and shouted, "I won't go! I refuse to go!"

"Very well, Sturgeon," replied his brother, "if you won't go with me I will have to go alone."

"You have deserted me!" cried Sturgeon. "We will never be brothers again! I will go into the water and I will never return."

Sturgeon left his brother and went into the water where he has lived ever since.

Sturgeon's brother went alone to the place where the animals were assembled. When they saw him they asked him to try on the antlers. He tried them on and the antlers fit as if they had been made for him.

"You look fine," said Coyote. "They fit perfectly."

Coyote sent Sturgeon's brother to the mountains for three months to become fat. At the end of three months the hunters went to look for him.

"There he is!" they cried. "There's Elk! He's fat!"

They pursued him. After they had pursued him over only one mountain, they overtook him. He was found to be just right for food.

18

Sturgeon's brother was very happy for he had wanted to be chosen Elk.

"You are no longer Sturgeon's brother," Coyote said. "In the future you will be known as Elk. The Indians are near now. They will be good marksmen and they will only have to pursue Elk over one mountain. That is the way it shall be."

That is how the animals determined who was to be Elk.

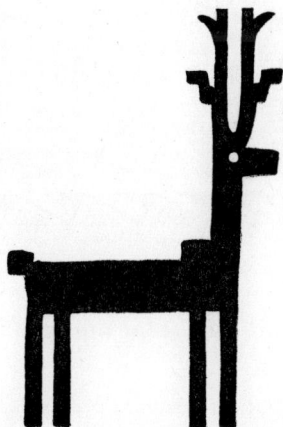

How Coyote Saved
the Three Timber Rabbit Brothers

THE THREE Timber Rabbit brothers lived together in a house in the woods.

The three brothers spent a great deal of time hunting, but they had never shot a deer.

One day the oldest brother said, "I'm going on a special hunting trip today. I've always wanted to get a deer and today I'm going to."

"Good luck," his two brothers said, as they waved good-by.

The oldest Timber Rabbit brother started through the

woods. He had not gone very far when he saw a deer ahead of him.

"I think I'm going to be lucky today," he thought, as he followed the deer through the woods.

He shot at the deer several times with his bow and arrow, but each time the deer escaped him. Timber Rabbit followed the deer on and on. Soon they were deep in the forest and the deer kept leading Timber Rabbit far, far away.

Finally, Timber Rabbit became very tired and he lay down to take a nap. When he awoke he was in a very strange place. He was puzzled.

"The deer must have brought me here," he thought, looking around him. "I wonder where I am. There seems to be food of all sorts, but I don't see anyone anywhere."

He looked around him very carefully again. Suddenly he said, "I know where I am! The deer has taken me beneath the water of the lake! How am I ever going to get out?"

Timber Rabbit was frightened, but he thought, "Surely my brothers will come and rescue me."

When Timber Rabbit did not return home after several days his brothers became very anxious. The next to the oldest Timber Rabbit brother started out to find him. He had not gone far into the woods when he, too, saw a deer. He was excited for he too had wanted to shoot a deer for a long time. He shot at it several times, but each time the deer escaped. He followed the deer on and on and he was led far, far into the woods. Finally he became tired and he

21

lay down to sleep for a while. When he awoke he found that he was in a very strange place.

"Where am I?" he wondered. "This seems to be beneath the lake. The deer must have brought me here."

He looked around him and then he saw his older brother.

"Brother!" the oldest Timber Rabbit cried. "So you, too, have been led to this place."

The two brothers were very glad to see each other. There was plenty of food and they were not hungry, but they could not see how they were going to escape.

"I don't think we'll ever get out," the oldest brother said sadly.

"There seems to be no way of escape," the second brother answered. "I'm afraid we'll have to stay here always."

Now there was only the youngest Timber Rabbit brother at home. He thought he knew where his brothers were. But he needed help so he went to see Coyote.

"If you think your brothers are beneath the lake, we will need a magic power to get them out," Coyote told him, after he had listened to his story.

"How will we get a magic power?" asked Timber Rabbit.

"Come with me," Coyote said, leading the way into the woods. "I'll show you."

First, Coyote made a bone arrow. Then he shot the arrow at a tree. The tree fell and Coyote said, "Now, Timber Rabbit, I have a magic power. I will be able to kill the deer."

22

"Let's go then," Timber Rabbit answered. "I'm worried about my brothers."

Timber Rabbit and Coyote started out through the woods. Very soon they saw the deer ahead of them. It was the same deer that had led the two oldest Timber Rabbit brothers away.

The deer looked behind to see if Timber Rabbit was following him. He saw Coyote. He was frightened for he was afraid of Coyote. "Coyote will kill me if I'm not careful," he thought, trying to hide behind a large tree.

Coyote, however, had seen the deer. He shot an arrow at him but did not hit the deer. Coyote decided to shoot once more and he shot at the deer with his bone arrow head. This time the deer cried out in pain.

"Coyote has killed me!" he cried, as he fell to the ground.

"I've killed the deer!" shouted Coyote.

Timber Rabbit and Coyote went on their way. Coyote had his magic power and they soon found the lake to which the deer had led the two oldest Timber Rabbit brothers. It was a very large lake. The youngest Timber Rabbit brother was discouraged when he saw it.

"How can we ever get my brothers out?" he asked Coyote. "It's so large we won't even know where to look for them."

"I still have the magic power I obtained when I felled the tree," Coyote told him. "Look!"

Coyote raised his hand and instantly the lake dried up. In a few minutes the two oldest Timber Rabbit brothers were walking toward them.

The three brothers threw their arms around each other. They were very happy to be together again. The youngest brother explained how Coyote had obtained the magic power, killed the deer, and dried up the lake.

"In the future," Coyote said, "there will be no lake here. Some day the Indians will be living in the land and this sort of thing must never happen to them. When the Indians come they will hunt and shoot deer for food. Deer will never be dangerous again."

It has been that way ever since.

Coyote and Snowbird

COYOTE traveled in many lands. Wherever he went he found many good things. He traded his possessions to obtain all the good things that he saw and then they became Coyote's.

One day, during his travels, he saw Grouse seated on the ground. Coyote watched him and saw that he was doing something very nice—something that Coyote had never seen before. He was tossing his eyes into the air!

Coyote approached him. "Let's exchange eyes, Grouse!" he cried.

"No!" answered Grouse. "I don't want to give you my eyes. I want them myself."

Coyote did not give up. He pleaded and pleaded with Grouse.

"Please!" he begged. "Please give me your eyes!"

"Oh, very well," Grouse replied. "I may as well let you have them. At dawn go to the summit of the mountain. Then you, too, will be able to toss up your eyes."

At dawn Coyote went to the summit of the mountain. When the sun rose he tossed up his eyes exactly as Grouse had done.

Soon Buzzard came that way. Quietly, he watched Coyote.

"Mmm," he said. "Coyote is doing something very nice with his eyes. I'd like to be able to do the same thing."

Buzzard was very pleased and watched Coyote for a long time.

"I think I'll come back again tomorrow," he said to himself.

The next sunrise Coyote came back to the summit of the mountain. Buzzard followed close behind him. Coyote tossed his eyes into the air. Quickly, Buzzard seized the eyes and flew away with them.

"My eyes!" cried Coyote. "My eyes are gone!"

Without his eyes Coyote knew he could never get down the mountain again. Then he remembered that he had seen many flowers growing around him. He reached out his hand and picked two flowers. For a while he could see very well. But he had not gone far when the flowers wilted and Coyote could no longer see. He made another pair of eyes from flowers. When they wilted and dried he made new eyes. He had eyes of every color—blue, yellow, red—all the colors there were. But none of the flowers lasted long and finally he had used all the flowers growing on the mountain but one. He made eyes with the last flower and traveled on.

He had not gone far when he met Bird Boy coming along the path.

"What are you doing on the mountain?" Coyote asked Bird Boy.

"I'm hunting mountain goats," Bird Boy answered. "There are supposed to be many mountain goats around here but so far I haven't seen any."

Coyote pointed ahead of him. "There are some over there," he said.

Bird Boy looked where Coyote was pointing. "I don't see any mountain goats," he replied.

"Your eyes must be very bad," Coyote answered. "I can see them very plainly. I have very good eyes. Would you like to trade eyes with me?"

"Oh, yes!" Bird Boy answered, eagerly. "Your eyes must be very good if you can see the mountain goats. Let's trade, please!"

Coyote gave Bird Boy his flower eyes and Bird Boy gave Coyote his eyes. Coyote was very grateful and he said to Bird Boy, "In the future you will no longer be just Bird Boy. The Indians are coming to the land soon and they will call you Snowbird. There will always be thickets for you to live in, and you will not need your eyes to hunt mountain goats for in the future you will always fly in low places."

Snowbirds have lived in thickets ever since.

27

Skunk and Coyote

ONCE Coyote went to visit Skunk for a few days. The weather was very cold and neither Skunk nor Coyote went outdoors to hunt. Soon they had eaten all the food in the house and they were very hungry.

"I think I know how we can eat," Coyote said.

"How?" Skunk asked.

"You must pretend that you are ill. I'll whiten you so that the animals will think that you are very ill. Then I will bring the animals here and we won't have to go hunting. I'll go first thing in the morning."

When morning came Coyote went to the five Black Tailed Deer brothers. He ran through the woods and knocked on their door.

"Good morning, Coyote," said Black Tailed Deer, opening the door. "Won't you come in?"

"Oh, no," answered Coyote, "my friend, Skunk, is very ill. He wants to see you. Will you come with me?"

"Of course," Black Tailed Deer said. "I'll tell my brothers. Will you wait?"

"No, I think I'd better go on ahead. I shouldn't leave Skunk any longer than necessary," said Coyote.

"Very well, Coyote. We'll be there very soon."

Coyote ran quickly back through the woods to Skunk's house.

"Get ready!" he told Skunk. "They're on their way!"

Skunk moaned loudly. "Ow! Ow! Ow!" he cried as if he were in great pain.

When the Deer brothers came, they were alarmed. "What can we do for him?" they asked.

"Oh, Deer!" moaned Skunk. "Take me outside! Please take me outside!"

"He wants to go outside," said Coyote. "I think we'd better take him. You carry his legs and I'll take his head."

They carried Skunk outside. When they were outside, Skunk discharged his musk at them. Every one of the Deer brothers fell dead.

Skunk and Coyote dressed the deer and there was a great quantity of food for them. But the meat did not last very long. Soon it was all gone and Skunk and Coyote were hungry again.

"Tomorrow I'll get the five Elk brothers," said Coyote. "You must pretend to be ill again."

Coyote went to the five Elk brothers.

"Skunk is seriously ill," he told them. "He's asking for you. Will you come back with me?"

"Why, certainly," replied Elk. "I'll get my brothers. Will you wait?"

"No, I must get back at once," Coyote answered. "Skunk doesn't like to be left alone."

Coyote ran back through the woods and reached Skunk before the Elk brothers arrived.

"They're coming!" he said to Skunk. "Get ready!"

"Ow! Ow! Ow!" cried Skunk as if he were suffering greatly.

"He does seem very ill," said Elk. "What can we do to help?"

"Take me out, Elk!" groaned Skunk. "Take me out!"

"He wants to go outside," explained Coyote. "You take his legs and I'll take his head."

They carried Skunk outside. When they were outside, Skunk discharged his musk. The five Elk brothers fell dead.

Coyote and Skunk sharpened their knives and butchered the elk. There was a great quantity of meat which they dried and ate. Soon, however, all the food was gone.

"Now I'll get the five Antlerless Deer brothers," Coyote said.

Coyote went to the house of the five Antlerless Deer brothers.

"You must come with me immediately," Coyote told them. "Skunk is very ill and he wants to see you."

"We'll come at once," said Antlerless Deer.

Coyote ran on ahead to warn Skunk.

"They're on their way! Get ready!" Coyote cried, as he ran into Skunk's house.

"Ow! Ow! Ow!" moaned Skunk.

The Antlerless Deer looked at Coyote with alarm.

"He seems to be much worse," Coyote said. "We must take him outside. You take his legs and I'll take his head."

When they were outside Skunk discharged his musk. All the Antlerless Deer fell dead in a heap.

Coyote and Skunk butchered the deer, sliced the meat, dried it, and brought it into the house. Soon they had eaten all of it.

"All of our food is gone," Coyote said. "I'll go get the Mountain Goat brothers."

Coyote went to the five Mountain Goat brothers.

"Skunk is ill," he told them. "He wants to see you. Will you come with me?"

"We'll come at once," Mountain Goat answered. "I'll bring my brothers."

Coyote ran on ahead to warn Skunk.

"They're coming!" he shouted. "Get ready!"

"Ow! Ow! Ow!" groaned Skunk. "I'm getting very weak. Take me outside! Take me outside!"

"He wants to go outside," Coyote explained to the mountain goats. "He'll be better outside. You carry his legs and I'll carry his head."

They carried Skunk outside. He discharged his musk and the five Mountain Goat brothers fell dead.

Coyote and Skunk sharpened their knives, butchered the five Mountain Goat brothers, and lived on the meat for some time. Then it, too, was all gone.

"This time I'll have to get the five Antlered Deer brothers," Coyote told Skunk.

The next day Coyote went to the home of the five Antlered Deer brothers.

"Skunk is very ill," he said to Antlered Deer, who opened the door. "He's been calling for you and your brothers. Will you come with me?"

"Just as soon as I tell my brothers," Antlered Deer replied. "Will you wait?"

"Oh, no," Coyote said hastily. "I must get back as quickly as possible."

"Very well, Coyote," answered Antlered Deer. "You may expect us very soon."

Coyote ran on ahead and reached Skunk's house first.

"They're coming!" he shouted to Skunk. "Get ready! They're coming!"

"Ow! Ow! Ow!" moaned Skunk, when the deer came. "Help me, Deer! I want to go outside! Please take me outside!"

"He wants to go outside," Coyote told the Antlered Deer. "You take his feet and I'll take his head."

They carried Skunk outside. But the Antlered Deer were wise. They knew what Skunk had in mind. Just as Skunk was about to discharge his musk, the oldest Antlered Deer brother stabbed him with his antler. He picked him up on his horn and ran away with him.

The Antlered Deer brothers carried Skunk to a rock cliff and hurled him down below.

"You have killed many people," they said to Skunk.

32

"The Indians will be living in the land soon. In the future you will never again be dangerous, nor will you be able to kill people with your musk."

Skunk has not been dangerous since that day. Nor has he been very popular.

How Coyote Defeated Wood Rat

ONE DAY Coyote and the rest of the animals were playing games. They were having a very good time when Wood Rat and his two sons appeared.

Wood Rat insisted upon playing and he won the game each time. He did not win fairly, however, for Wood Rat cheated.

Coyote was angry. When the game was over he said to his son, "Come with me—we're going to follow Wood Rat."

Coyote and his son went down to the river and into a canoe. The river was full of rapids, but Coyote was ready. He had brought a huge hollow log. While the canoe was passing through the rapids, Coyote and his son lay inside the log. When they had passed through the rapids they came out of the hollow log. In this way they rode dry and unhurt through the rapids.

Wood Rat was watching and he could not understand it. "Coyote must be very powerful," he said. "They have passed through five rapids and they are unhurt."

Wood Rat wanted to kill Coyote, and when Coyote and his son reached his home, which was a rock in the water, he asked them both to come inside.

The house was cold and dark. There was no firewood to burn for Wood Rat burned only bones.

"I'm sorry it's so cold here," Wood Rat apologized, "but I think we'll soon have a fire."

Wood Rat had not fooled Coyote. He knew that if Wood Rat caught him and his son he would use them for fuel. Coyote still had the log with him and he and his son crept inside.

Wood Rat was angry, but he held his temper for he had still another plan.

"I'm very hungry," he said. "Perhaps your son will go down to the rapids and spear some salmon for us."

Wood Rat had turned his own son into a Chinook salmon, hoping that the trick would deceive Coyote's son and he would be killed in the falls.

Coyote remained in the log, but his son came out and went down to the rapids. He paddled in his canoe to the cascades. Near the falls he saw a large Chinook salmon.

"There's a Chinook salmon!" he cried. "Now we can eat!" He speared the salmon and then clubbed it to death.

When Wood Rat saw that Coyote's son had killed his

35

son he was very angry. His trick had not turned out as he had planned. There must be something else he could do.

But Coyote had slipped out of the log and was waiting by the river for his son to return.

"Hurry!" he called out as his son paddled into sight. "Let's go quickly before Wood Rat discovers I have left his house!"

Coyote jumped into the canoe with his son and they paddled hard. They passed one fall and rested from paddling. Wood Rat was following them.

"He's discovered I'm gone," Coyote told his son. "Paddle hard!"

When they reached the next rapids they stopped to rest again. Wood Rat was still following them. They paddled on to the next rapids and again stopped to rest. Wood Rat was finding it hard to catch up with them. Coyote and his son went on to the next rapids and reached the falls. They had passed through all five rapids safely. Wood Rat could not catch them. Coyote had defeated him and Wood Rat knew it.

"Never again will you be dangerous to anyone," Coyote called to Wood Rat. "The Indians will be here soon and in the future you will pick up food where you can find it and never kill anyone again. Your name will be Wood Rat for all time. I, Coyote, name you."

That is how Coyote spoke and that is the way it is today.

Coyote and the Mischievous Weasel

ONE DAY when Coyote was traveling he met Weasel.

"Take me with you, Coyote," Weasel said. "Please take me with you!"

"I don't think I should, Weasel." Coyote hesitated. "You're a very mischievous fellow, and you'll get us into trouble if I take you with me."

"Please!" Weasel pleaded. "I promise to keep out of trouble. Please take me with you!"

"All right, Weasel," Coyote agreed. "But see that you behave yourself."

Coyote and Weasel started down the road. Soon they came to two women who were digging roots by a lake.

"Let's ask the two women to come along," suggested Weasel.

"No!" answered Coyote. "The women belong to a Dangerous Being. Come along and forget about them."

Weasel paid no attention to Coyote's warning and walked over to the two women.

Coyote was angry. He turned and walked away.

Soon Weasel caught up with him. "I talked to the two women," he boasted.

"That was very foolish," Coyote answered. "I told you they were the wives of a Dangerous Being. He'll probably follow us now. Hurry!"

Quickly, they walked on. Coyote looked behind. Coming rapidly toward them was the Dangerous Being.

"What did I tell you!" Coyote demanded angrily. "The Dangerous Being is following us—if we're not careful he'll swallow us. Hurry!" He took Weasel by the hand and they started to run very fast.

Weasel was frightened and he started to cry. By now the Dangerous Being had nearly caught up with them.

"Over there!" said Coyote, pointing to a hole in a cliff. "We'll hide inside the rock."

It was too late. The Dangerous Being caught up with them and he swallowed them, rock and all.

Inside the Dangerous Being, Weasel said, "I'm going to try and get out, Coyote. I want to find out what sort of Dangerous Being has swallowed us."

"Be careful!" Coyote warned. "You've caused enough trouble."

Very carefully Weasel crawled out of the mouth of the

Dangerous Being and looked around. He was pleased with what he saw.

"This is very good," he said, as he crawled back inside to Coyote. "The Dangerous Being is a large rattlesnake. I think we can kill him."

"There's no way to kill him," Coyote said.

"There must be some way to kill him," Weasel answered. "I'm going outside again."

Weasel went outside again. "Mmm," he said, looking carefully at the large rattlesnake, "I think the Dangerous Being is already dead. I'll go back and tell Coyote."

Weasel crawled inside again. "The snake is dead," he said. "He must have choked on the rock he swallowed with us. Let's skin him."

"Very well," agreed Coyote.

Coyote and Weasel crawled out of the snake's mouth. They peeled the skin from the snake, rolled it up, and continued on their journey. Coyote carried the rolled-up skin. After they had walked some distance, Weasel said, "Let me carry the skin awhile, Coyote."

"No," Coyote answered. "I can't trust you."

Weasel coaxed and finally Coyote agreed.

Weasel carried the skin. They had not gone very far when Weasel dropped behind Coyote.

"I'll give Coyote a scare," he thought. He loosened the pack with the skin and dressed in it, pulling it on like a shirt. Then he rattled softly like a rattlesnake. Coyote paid no attention. Weasel rattled louder. Coyote paid no attention. "He's being mischievous again," he thought. "I'll not act frightened. I'll frighten Weasel instead."

Turning quickly he lifted Weasel off the ground. Weasel was frightened.

"Coyote, save me!" he cried. "The Dangerous Being has returned to life and he's lifting me into the air! Please save me!"

Coyote dropped him to the ground. "You're a rascal, Weasel," he said. "Give me the skin—I'll carry it myself."

Coyote took the skin and they walked on. They came to a little brook.

"We'll camp here overnight," Coyote said.

"What's the name of this country?" Weasel asked, looking around with interest.

"I'm not going to tell you," Coyote said.

"But I want to learn the name of this country," insisted Weasel. He coaxed and coaxed.

"Oh, all right," Coyote said. "But if you get us into any more trouble we'll not remain together."

"I won't," Weasel promised.

"The name of this country is Tyigh Valley, Oregon," Coyote said.

Weasel laughed. "That's a fine name," he said. He ran to get some water and he shouted, "Tyigh! Tyigh! Tyigh!"

"Don't repeat that name!" shouted Coyote angrily. "Tyigh is another name for rain. If you repeat the name again it will rain and there'll be a flood."

Weasel paid no attention. "Tyigh! Tyigh! Tyigh!" he shouted.

It started to rain. The water of the creek overflowed and reached them. In the darkness Weasel found a piece of pine bark. He lay down on it and tried to sleep but the water soon reached him and after a while he drifted away on the bark.

"Help me, Coyote!" Weasel cried, as he drifted away on the bark. "Help me!"

"No, indeed!" called Coyote. "You had your chance, Weasel, and I warned you. You'll always be a rascal and you'll always be careless about everything. When the Indians come to live in the land they will name you Weasel, the rascal."

That is the way it has always been.

Coyote's Adventures
with Dangerous Beings

THERE WAS a Dangerous Being in the river. It had killed many people. The canoes on the river were gulped down by the River Monster, people and all. The Dangerous Being had a dog and the dog had a spy. The spy was Kingfisher.

When Coyote heard about the River Monster he said, "I'll kill him! I'll make a raft and the monster will choke on it!"

Coyote made a raft. He made a very large raft of Douglas fir. He put the raft in the river and floated downstream on it. But Coyote did not succeed in his plans to kill the monster, for he had not gone far before the Dangerous Being swallowed Coyote, raft, and all.

Moon and his brother, Sun, saw what happened.

"We'll have to save Coyote," Sun said. "Coyote's raft was made from Douglas fir. We'll make a canoe that will cut and tear the Dangerous Being apart. We'll make a canoe with a sharp-edged prow."

"Let's make it at once," said Moon. "There's no time to lose."

Sun and Moon went down to the edge of the river and made a canoe. Then they looked for Kingfisher.

"There he is!" said Moon. "Over in that tree watching us."

"Come here, Kingfisher," called Sun. "We want to show you something."

Kingfisher was curious. He flew over to Sun and Moon.

"What do you have to show me?" he asked.

Moon showed him red, green, and white paint. "Do you like it?" he asked.

"It's nice," Kingfisher answered without much interest.

"Your feathers aren't very bright, Kingfisher," Sun said. "You're really quite dull compared to some of the other birds."

Kingfisher considered this for a moment. "What can I do about it?" he asked.

"We could paint you," Moon suggested. "How would you like to be red, green, and white?"

"You mean you could make me red, green, and white?" Kingfisher asked with interest.

"Certainly," replied Moon. "If you promise to go away

43

and have nothing more to do with the Dangerous Being in the river, we'll paint your feathers red, green, and white."

Kingfisher was delighted. "I promise," he said. "I'll fly away and never see the Dangerous Being again."

Sun and Moon painted Kingfisher's feathers and he flew away as he had promised. Then they killed the Dangerous Being's dog and rode on in their canoe.

"Paddle hard!" Sun said. "We must hit the Dangerous Being and save Coyote!"

The River Monster saw them coming. He opened his mouth to swallow them, but Sun and Moon crashed into him with their canoe with the sharp-edged prow.

Out came Coyote. Also, all the other animals the Dangerous Being had swallowed. Some were still alive, others were dead. Sun and Moon stepped back and forth over those who were dead and the dead revived and became well and returned to their homes.

Coyote thanked Sun and Moon for killing the River Monster.

Then he went on his way. After a while he saw a house. An old man was sitting in front of it. The old man was Wild Cherry Bark.

"Where are you going?" he asked Coyote.

"I'm on my way to the buffalo country," Coyote replied.

"You'll never reach the buffalo country," Wild Cherry Bark said. "There's a monster nearby that you'll never be able to pass."

"I'm not afraid," answered Coyote. "I've just killed a monster—no monster can ever kill me."

44

"Indeed?" inquired Wild Cherry Bark. "What monster did you kill?"

"I killed the River Swallowing Monster. No monster can kill me," Coyote repeated boastfully...

"You may not be so successful this time," Wild Cherry Bark told Coyote. "This monster is far more dangerous than the River Swallowing Monster. You'll never pass it."

"I'll pass it all right," Coyote said, quite sure of his power.

"Very well," replied Wild Cherry Bark, "if you're so certain that you can pass this monster, I'll get some wild cherry bark for you. You may use it for any purpose you wish."

Wild Cherry Bark went into the house. When he came out he had a ball of bark in his hand. Before Coyote could move, Wild Cherry Bark struck him with it. Coyote fell down, and Wild Cherry Bark tied him up so that his legs were entirely wrapped with the cherry bark. Coyote took out his knife and cut at the bark. At last he was free. As Coyote got to his feet Wild Cherry Bark fell down and died. Wild Cherry Bark, although he walked and talked, was really only a large piece of cherry bark. When Coyote cut at the bark in which he had been tied he also killed Wild Cherry Bark.

Coyote burst into laughter. "Ha! Ha! Ha!" he laughed. "Wild Cherry Bark couldn't kill me! No one can kill me!"

He traveled on.

Soon he saw the monster that Wild Cherry Bark had warned him about. He was a very large monster and he was sitting in the middle of a valley. He was so large that he

45

nearly touched the mountains on both sides of the valley.

Coyote pulled grass and made himself a grass garment. He found five hazel ropes and with the hazel ropes he tied himself to the mountain side. He turned toward the Dangerous Being, which turned out to be a sucking monster.

"Let's have a contest," Coyote called to the monster. "Let's suck air!"

"Who's shouting at me?" the monster asked.

He looked all around, but he could not see Coyote for he was covered with grass and tied to the side of the mountain. Coyote shouted again. The monster looked around again. Still he could not see Coyote. Again Coyote shouted. This time when Coyote opened his mouth the monster saw him.

"There you are!" he said. "All right, we'll have a contest. You begin."

"No!" answered Coyote. "You begin—you're the one who is supposed to be dangerous."

"No!" shouted the monster. "You started this. You challenged me to an air-sucking contest and you have to begin."

Coyote stood up. "Very well," he said. "I'll begin."

Coyote sucked toward the monster. There was a strong wind and the monster was pulled nearly to Coyote's mouth. The monster was frightened. Whoever had challenged him to an air-sucking contest was very powerful. He sucked toward Coyote. One of the hazel ropes that held Coyote to the mountain side broke. Only four ropes held Coyote now.

"All right!" cried the monster. "It's your turn now."

Coyote sucked toward the monster so long that again one of the hazel ropes broke. Now there were only three

46

ropes holding him to the mountain. The monster sucked again. Coyote did not bend far this time, but another of the hazel ropes broke and there were only two still holding him. Coyote was getting short of breath, but he sucked once more toward the monster. Another rope broke. There was just one rope left now. The monster sucked toward Coyote. The last hazel rope broke and Coyote was sucked inside of the monster.

Inside of the monster Coyote looked around. The monster was so large that his interior was much like a house. There was food and Coyote ate. After he had eaten he took out his fire-making tools and made a large fire.

The monster became very ill. "It must be Coyote I've swallowed," he thought. "I'd better speak to him."

"I didn't know it was you I had swallowed, Coyote," the monster called. "I'm sorry I swallowed you. You may come out and go away."

"No, indeed!" Coyote called back. "I'm going to stay."

Coyote took out some dry sticks from his pocket and made an even larger fire.

The monster became very ill this time. He groaned in pain.

"Please go away, Coyote!" he called. "Please go away!"

"No, indeed!" answered Coyote. "You swallowed me and I intend to stay."

It was not long before the monster fell dead. Coyote went outside. He burst into laughter as he went on his way. "Ha! Ha! Ha!" he laughed. "I killed the monster! Nothing can kill me!"

Soon he met Fox.

47

"Where are you going, Coyote?" Fox asked.

"To the buffalo country," replied Coyote.

"Let me go with you," said Fox.

"All right, Fox," Coyote answered. "Come along."

"There is a Dangerous Being nearby," Fox said, as they traveled on. "I don't think you'll be able to pass it."

Coyote laughed. "I've killed many Dangerous Beings," he said. "I'm not afraid of this one. But who is this Dangerous Being?" he added.

"His name is Rock," Fox explained. "If you give him a blanket you may be able to pass. If you don't, he'll strike at you."

"I don't mind giving him a blanket," Coyote said.

Coyote and Fox soon reached Rock. They each gave him a blanket and were allowed to pass safely.

They had not gone far, however, when Coyote said to Fox, "You're a good-for-nothing, Fox! Why did you make me give Rock a blanket? We could probably have passed without giving him anything. I'm going back and get my blanket."

Fox was frightened. "Please don't go back, Coyote! He'll kill both of us!"

But Coyote laughed and ran back down the road. Suddenly, he heard a loud noise. Alarmed, he stopped and looked around. He saw that Rock was battering the hills and the ground to pieces. Coyote ran fast but Rock finally hit him. Coyote fell down on the road.

Rock then followed Fox. He overtook him, but Fox leaped aside. Rock rolled on and Fox ran on again. Soon Fox became tired. He heard someone shouting to him. The voice came from the lake—from the house of Grandfather Beaver.

"This way, Fox!" Grandfather Beaver shouted. "Come this way!"

Fox jumped into the lake and swam across. Rock saw him swimming to Grandfather Beaver's house. Rock leaped, fell into the water, and there he lay—a rock.

When Fox reached Grandfather Beaver's house, he said to him, "You're safe now, Fox. You can continue on your journey."

Fox thanked Grandfather Beaver and returned to look for Coyote. He found him lying on the ground, holding a blanket.

"I'm leaving you, Coyote," Fox said. "I'm afraid to travel with you any longer."

"Very well," replied Coyote. "But I'm not afraid. There's nothing that can hurt me."

Fox and Coyote separated and Coyote went far, far away.

"I must be in the buffalo country," Coyote said, when he saw a buffalo a short distance ahead of him.

The buffalo saw Coyote, too. Angrily, he started to chase him. Nearby, Coyote saw five Douglas fir trees. He ran very fast, reached the trees and climbed one of the first just as Buffalo overtook him.

Buffalo was very angry. He leaped at the fir, pierced it with his horns and the tree crashed to the ground. Coyote jumped to another fir. Buffalo pierced it with his horns and it, too, fell. Again the same thing happened.

"Now he'll kill me," Coyote thought fearfully. "There are only two more fir trees!"

Buffalo was furious. Again he leaped at the fir, caught it on his horn, and the tree gave way. Only one fir tree remained.

Coyote was terrified. "You've ruined your horns, Buffalo," he said. "They're no longer any good for anything. I'll make you a new pair of horns if you'd like."

"Do you know how to make horns?" Buffalo asked with interest.

"I can make very good horns," Coyote answered.

"Very well, then," said Buffalo. "Make me some new horns."

Coyote was still frightened and he remained in the tree.

"I'll not hurt you, Coyote," Buffalo said. "I can use some new horns—come down and make them."

Coyote was frightened, but he came down from the tree. He took the knot of a dead log and bending and pointing it well, he made one horn.

Buffalo looked at it. "That looks like a very fine horn," he said. "All right now, Coyote! Make another horn for me."

Coyote found another knot and made a second horn.

"Fine," said Buffalo. "Now perhaps you can remove these old horns from me."

"Yes, indeed!" said Coyote.

He removed Buffalo's old horns and fitted the new ones on him. They were fine horns and Buffalo was well pleased.

Coyote returned home safely.

Coyote's Adventures
in a New Land

ONE DAY Coyote decided to go far, far away on a journey. He traveled toward the north and into a country where he had never been before.

Along the way he found a black hornets' nest and he picked it up and took it with him. He had not gone far when he met the five Frog sisters. They were digging roots beside the road.

When they saw Coyote one of the sisters called to him, "Who are you and where did you come from?"

Coyote pretended not to hear and kept on walking.

Another sister called to him, "Who are you and where did you come from?"

Again he pretended not to hear and kept on walking.

"Where did you come from?" one of the sisters called again.

This time Coyote answered, "I came from the west—along the ocean coast," he said. "My name is Coyote. I'm well known in my own country."

"What are you carrying with you?" one of the Frog sisters asked, noticing the hornets' nest in Coyote's hand.

"Food," answered Coyote. "I'm carrying it with me in case I get hungry."

"Will you give us some food?" inquired one of the sisters. "We've been working hard and we're very hungry."

Coyote hesitated a moment. He was in a strange land and he was a little suspicious of the Frog sisters. But he replied, "Certainly. Come over to my side of the road and we'll all sit down and eat."

The five Frog sisters crossed the road and sat down. Coyote placed the hornets' nest in front of them.

"I haven't much food," he said, sitting down beside them, "so don't eat it too rapidly."

"We won't," the sisters promised.

The sisters reached for the hornets' nest which Coyote had told them was food. They were badly stung and they all fell unconscious along the road.

Coyote continued on his way, glad to be rid of the Frog sisters.

The Frog sisters were not unconscious long, however.

When they awoke they were very angry with Coyote for the trick he had played on them.

"The stranger who gave us the hornets' nest to eat should be punished," one of them said.

"I think so, too," agreed another sister. "What shall we do to him?"

"Let's sing our snow song. The snow will fall and the stranger will be cold and without shelter." They sang.

Suddenly it started to snow. It snowed hard and soon the countryside was completely covered. It was very cold.

Coyote shivered as he walked along. "Strange that it should start to snow," he thought. "A moment ago it was a nice day. Maybe I can find a place to keep warm until the snowstorm is over."

He looked around. Standing near was a fir tree with a large hole in it. He ran to the tree and stepped into the hole.

"It would be much warmer if the hole were closed," he said. "I wonder if I can make it close. I do not know the trees in this country—perhaps there's a special word to close holes in trees. I'll try. Close, Tree!" he said aloud. "Close!"

The hole in the tree immediately closed. It was warm inside and Coyote was pleased. "Now I wonder if I can make it open again. Open, Tree!" he said. "Open!"

The hole in the tree opened. Coyote was satisfied. He commanded the tree to close again and then he lay down and went to sleep.

When he awoke he was very hungry. He decided to go outside and look for food.

"Let me out, Tree!" he said to the hole in the tree.

He waited but the hole remained closed.

"I want to get out!" Coyote shouted. "Let me out!"

The hole remained closed.

Coyote was frightened. The tree had opened and closed at his command before. What was the matter now?

"What shall I do?" he wondered. "I want to go outside and I can't remember the word I used before." Suddenly he had an idea. "I'll call Black Woodpecker. He'll help me. Black Woodpecker!" he called loudly. "Make a hole in the tree for me!"

Coyote waited. Soon he heard a chopping noise on the outside of the tree.

"Is that you, Black Woodpecker?" Coyote called from inside the tree.

"No," a voice answered from the outside. "I am Yellow-hammer."

"Go away, Yellowhammer," Coyote said. "I called for Black Woodpecker. I'll call him again.

"Black Woodpecker!" Coyote called. "Make a hole in the tree for me!"

Soon he heard the sound of chopping on the outside of the tree.

"Is that you, Black Woodpecker?" he asked.

"No," a voice answered. "I am Sapsucker."

"Go away, Sapsucker," Coyote said. "I don't want you —I want Black Woodpecker. I'll call him again."

Sapsucker went away and Coyote called Woodpecker again. Soon he heard a chopping sound from the outside of the tree.

54

"Is that you, Black Woodpecker?" Coyote asked. "Did you come this time?"

"Yes, I came. I'm Black Woodpecker."

"Chop hard and make a big hole so I can get out," Coyote said.

Black Woodpecker chopped. The hole became larger and larger. Soon Coyote could see Black Woodpecker as he worked. He watched him silently.

"He has very fine feathers," Coyote thought. "I'd like to have them myself." Aloud, he said to Woodpecker, "Chop closer, Woodpecker."

Black Woodpecker obeyed. As he came closer Coyote pulled him toward him. Black Woodpecker was frightened. He pleaded with Coyote to free him. But Coyote held him closer. Black Woodpecker struggled to free himself and finally he slipped free of Coyote's hand.

"Please come back, Black Woodpecker," Coyote called after him. "I was only playing with you. Please come back!"

Black Woodpecker did not come back. Coyote was left by himself and the hole was not yet large enough for him to get out. He could get his head through the hole in the tree and that was all.

Coyote thought for a long time. "I know!" he exclaimed. "I'll take my body apart and then I can put each piece through the hole separately."

Coyote took off his arms, legs, and head and put them through the hole in the tree. Soon he was outside. He put his body together again and went on his way.

He had not traveled far when he saw a crowd of ani-

55

mals ahead of him. They were playing a game and having a very good time. Coyote wanted to play with them. He stepped up to Black Bear, one of the animals in the group.

"May I play with you?" he asked.

"No!" answered Black Bear, sternly. "We don't know you and only those who live in this country may play with us. Go back where you came from. We don't want you here."

The crowd was angry. When Coyote did not move they started to chase him, throwing stones at him. Coyote ran fast, but the other animals were close behind him.

"Go away!" they shouted angrily. "We don't want strangers in our country. Go away!"

Coyote was nearly out of breath. The crowd was close behind and he would soon be caught.

"I'll turn into a stick," he thought. "That will fool them!" Coyote suddenly disappeared.

"He's gone!" said Black Bear. "That's very strange—he was right in front of us a moment ago. Where could he have gone?"

"Here's a stick," one of the animals said, noticing the stick lying in the road. "Do you suppose he could have turned himself into a stick?"

"Oh, no," answered Black Bear. "Only very important and powerful persons have such magic power. He's probably hiding somewhere near—we may as well go back."

When they had gone Coyote turned back into himself. He started to run very fast. Soon he heard angry cries behind him.

"There he is again!" someone shouted. "He must have been hiding somewhere. Let's chase him away again!"

Coyote ran faster, but when he looked behind him he saw that the crowd had nearly caught up with him.

"I'll change myself into dirt this time," he said. Again Coyote disappeared.

"But he was right here," Black Bear protested. "Right here on this spot."

"There's nothing here now but dirt," one of the animals said. "We'll never find him—let's go back."

When they had gone Coyote changed back into himself. He started to run very fast. Again, one of the animals saw him.

"There he is again!" they shouted. "Let's get him this time!"

Coyote was frightened. This time they would surely catch him. They were very close behind him—closer than they had ever been.

"If my house would only appear by the stream ahead of me!" Coyote wished aloud.

As soon as he had said the words his house appeared by the side of the stream. Smoke came out of the chimney and a Chinook salmon was hanging outside of the house to dry.

Coyote entered the house and closed the door. When Black Bear knocked on the door he was sitting in front of the fire making a fish spear.

"Have you seen anyone around here?" Black Bear asked. "We're chasing a stranger who doesn't live in this country. Have you seen anyone pass?"

57

"Why, yes," Coyote answered, "just a few seconds ago someone passed by the house running very fast."

"That must have been the stranger!" Black Bear answered. "He can't have gotten very far. Come on," he said to the other animals who were waiting outside, "let's catch him!"

They never found Coyote. After it was dark he started back to the ocean coast he had come from. He was very grateful to be safe at home for he had had some narrow escapes on his journey to the country far to the north.

Coyote and Fox
Visit the Sioux Country

ONE DAY Coyote said to his friend, Fox, "Let's go on a long trip, Fox. Let's cross the mountains and plains and walk toward the east where the run rises."

Fox agreed and they started out. They traveled for many days. They crossed the mountains and the hills and started across the plains far to the east.

One day as they were walking along they passed a huckleberry bush and a pine tree.

"Stop!" they heard someone call.

"What was that?" Fox asked, looking around. "I don't see anyone."

"We're right beside you," a voice said. "I'm Huckleberry."

"I'm Pine Cone," said another voice. "We want to warn you about the country ahead. Not far away you'll meet a Dangerous Being who has two dogs named Wahmu and Tililqa. You'll not find it easy to pass him."

"If we only had two dogs ourselves!" Coyote said.

"We'll help you," Huckleberry said.

"How can you help?" asked Coyote.

"Watch!" said Pine Cone.

Instantly, Huckleberry and Pine Cone became two dogs. Coyote and Fox were glad to have the two dogs and they continued their journey. Coyote was not afraid for where he came from he was considered a very powerful being.

It wasn't long before they met the Dangerous Being.

"Be careful!" Coyote cried. "We, also, have two dogs and one of our dogs may bite and kill you."

"What are their names?" asked the Dangerous Being.

"Wahmu and Tililqa," replied Coyote.

"Mine are named the very same!" said the Dangerous Being.

"Why not let them play together then?" suggested Coyote.

"Oh, no!" protested the Dangerous Being.

Coyote insisted. "Let them play!" he shouted.

The Dangerous Being feared Coyote and he agreed. "Very well," he said. "Our dogs will play."

Both Wahmus played together and the Wahmu of Coyote killed the Wahmu of the Dangerous Being.

"Now let the two Tililqas play!" Coyote said.

60

The Dangerous Being was frightened and he agreed. "Very well," he said.

The dogs played and fought and the dog belonging to the Dangerous Being was killed. Coyote and Fox were able to pass and to continue their trip.

After a few days they came to a place where a great crowd was gathered. The leader of the crowd was Wolf. He was a cruel leader and he had killed many of his followers. He ran foot races with them and when he won he chopped off the head of the one with whom he had raced. He was very powerful and he won every race.

When Wolf saw Coyote and Fox standing at the edge of the crowd he walked over to them and said, "What are you two doing in this country?"

"We're on a trip," explained Coyote. "We're just passing through the country."

"Would you like to race with me?" asked Wolf.

"Yes," Coyote answered. "We will race with you. You race with Wolf first, Fox."

"Very well," agreed Fox.

Fox and Wolf raced. At first it looked as if Fox might win, but Wolf soon caught up with him. Fox lost the race and Wolf cut off his head.

Coyote was worried. "I suppose I'll be killed, too," he thought.

"It's your turn now to race with me," Wolf said. "Let's begin!"

Coyote and Wolf raced. Coyote, too, lost the race.

"Hurry!" Wolf shouted to the watching animals. "Chop off his head!"

They chopped off Coyote's head. The heads of Fox and Coyote were thrown down close together and Wolf and his followers left.

During the night Coyote awoke and by his magic he joined his head to his body again. Then he did the same thing for Fox.

"We'd better leave this country," Coyote said to Fox. "You and I must part and in the future we will always travel separately. The Indians will soon be coming to live in the land and this country will be the land whose people will be named the Sioux Indians. According to my law that is the way it will be. Go now, Fox. Go to the mountains where you will always live. I, myself, will travel in every land. That is how I, Coyote, make the law."

Fox and Coyote parted, for that was the way Coyote ordained it.

Coyote's Last Adventure

THE LAND was ready for the Indians. The streams and mountains were named, the rivers and lakes were full of fish, there was a day and a night and there was a spring and fall, and fire and water. There were no more Dangerous Beings in the land and the animals had become animals who no longer talked. Now that Coyote's work was finished, he expected the Indians very soon. He was sure that they would be pleased with the land that he had prepared for them.

One day he went for a walk. Suddenly—as if he had come out of nowhere—a man appeared on the path ahead of him.

"Where are you going?" asked the stranger.

"I'm going for a walk," Coyote answered.

"Are you hungry?" the man asked.

"Oh, yes!" Coyote replied eagerly. He had never seen the man before, but he was not afraid for the stranger had offered him food.

"Very well," replied the man. He looked around. "Let's eat over there by the stream," he suggested.

The man unfolded a mat which he spread on the ground.

"Sit down," he said to Coyote.

Coyote sat down by the stream.

"Now close your eyes tightly," said the man.

Coyote closed his eyes tightly. The man prayed and then he said to Coyote, "Now look!"

Coyote looked. The mat was covered with every variety of food. Coyote was delighted. They both ate and after they had finished their meal the man said, "Have you had enough to eat?"

"Yes, indeed," Coyote answered. "I've had plenty to eat."

"Then close your eyes tightly," the man told him.

Coyote closed his eyes. The man prayed and then he said, "Now look!"

Coyote looked. The food was no longer there. The man rolled up the mat and said to Coyote, "I always do this when I'm hungry."

Coyote was impressed. He wished he had the mat so he could do the same thing. "I'll kill him," he thought, "and I'll be able to do the same thing."

The strange man knew what Coyote was thinking. "He wants to kill me," he thought. "I shall not stop him, but he will be punished."

Coyote killed the man who had fed him. He took his breeches, waist, and moccasins. Then he went on his way.

Soon he came to another stream. "I'm hungry," he said. "I think I'll eat again."

He spread out the mat and prayed exactly as the strange man had done. In an instant there was food on the mat. He ate until he could eat no more. Then he closed his eyes, prayed and the food was no longer there. Coyote went on far, far away.

Suddenly—as if he had come out of nowhere—a man appeared on the path ahead of him. "Strange," thought Coyote, "he looks very much like the man I killed."

"Where are you going?" asked the man.

"I'm going for a walk," answered Coyote.

"I'll go with you," replied the man.

"Very well," agreed Coyote.

The man and Coyote went on together. After a while they came to a mountain.

"I shall say good-by to you now," the man told Coyote. "Where I'm going you must not follow."

The man started to climb the mountain. Coyote watched him for a moment. "I'm going to follow him!" he thought. "I want to know where he's going where I must not follow." He looked at the mountain. "It looks like a difficult mountain to climb," he said. "How will I get over it?" Then he had an idea. "I'll sing and then I'll be able to climb

65

the mountain!" He started to sing. "Raise me above at once!" he sang. Instantly, Coyote reached the top of the mountain and followed the man.

Soon he came to a lake. He could see the man ahead who was having no difficulty at all crossing the large lake. "I'll sing again," Coyote thought. "That'll help me across the lake." Coyote sang, "Get me across the lake at once!" Instantly, he was across the large lake.

The man looked back and saw Coyote close behind him. "Coyote is too powerful," he thought. He went on with Coyote close behind him. After a while he stopped. Coyote stopped, too. It was a very strange place—Coyote had never seen anything like it before. Where could he be, he wondered. It didn't look like the rest of the land.

The strange man spoke to him. "Come here, Coyote!" he said sternly.

Coyote looked at the man closely. Then he recognized him. "Why, he is the man I killed!" he said in astonishment. Coyote was frightened for the strange man must be very powerful, too.

"Yes, Coyote," said the man. "I am the same man you thought you had killed. I have been testing you. But you failed the test—first, by trying to kill me and then, by following me here. You should never have followed me here, for this is the Land of the Dead. No one will ever see this land until he is dead. In the future, when the Indians die, they will come here. You must go back where you came from and you may never come to this land again. No, not even when you die. That will be your punishment for following me. Go back now to that other land. For as long as that land is there you will be there, too."

That is how it was ordained for Coyote. He is no longer Coyote, the person of the myth age of long ago, but the animal, coyote. That is how coyote is today.

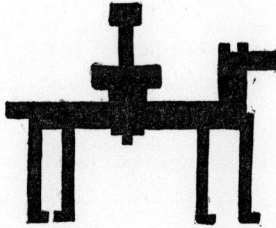

Sources used

PROFESSOR MELVILLE JACOBS of the Department of Anthropology of the University of Washington has a large collection of myths and tales obtained from many Indian natives of Oregon and Washington. For this book I have used his translations of a few myths dictated to him by several elderly Indians, later deceased, among them Joe Hunt, a Klikitat Sahaptin of southern central Washington; Jim Yoke, an Upper Cowlitz Sahaptin of western Washington; Annie Peterson, a Coos of Empire, Oregon, and some others.

The publications by Professor Jacobs which contain the original texts and translations are *Northwest Sahaptin Texts, 1,* University of Washington Publications in Anthropology, Vol. 2, No. 6, Seattle, 1929; *Northwest Sahaptin Texts,* Columbia University Contributions to Anthropology, Vol. 19, Pts. 1 and 2, New York, 1934-1936; *Coos Myth Texts,* University of Washington Publications in Anthropology, Vol. 8, No. 2, Seattle, 1940; and *Kalapuya Texts,* University of Washington Publications in Anthropology, Vol. 11, Seattle, 1945.

In order to make the stories I have selected more suitable for children, and intelligible to them, many liberties have been taken with the translations as published by Professor Jacobs. This has been done with his approval.

CORINNE RUNNING

Origins of these stories

THIS BOOK constitutes a small collection of myths culled from a few of my technical publications on the folklore of American Indians of Oregon and Washington. The myths were originally noted in the phonetic transcription employed by students when writing American Indian languages at the dictation of their native informants. Some of the myths adapted here are still being told by Sahaptin-speaking Indians, especially the Upper Cowlitz and Klikitat groups in the south central parts of the state of Washington. A few stories once told in the nearly extinct Coos and Kalapuya languages of western Oregon are also included.

Corinne Running, who suggested using my texts for a popularized volume of Pacific Northwest stories, has been sensitively appreciative of those qualities in the esoteric oral literatures which make them entertaining to non-Indian young people. She has chosen only myths which will be interesting to a larger audience than the students who seek out anthropological monographs, and has changed and supplemented the original versions in many ways for the sake of her special audience. Most changes were judged necessary for non-Indian children. Translation into English of course involved also the loss of stylistic features which are many and complex in the Indians' recitations of myths in their native languages and cultural settings.

Myths served several purposes among the Indians of the Pacific

Northwest. During the winter season they provided months of entertainment. The myths also amounted to an orally transmitted encyclopedia of community history and tradition. They professed to account for the supposedly long period of mythic time before the Indian people entered the country. Myths such as these accounted for the origins of crafts, arts, religious beliefs, and social institutions; they explained the physical characteristics and habits of birds, animals, and fish; they explained rivers, valleys, mountains, and other natural phenomena. Northwestern Indians heard stories such as these from their earliest years, often told by masters of the art of folklore. Adult Indians even now could repeat their people's stories almost verbatim, though with embellishments, individual colorings, and creative changes and additions which make a variety of versions current in each community. Many native audiences of the northwestern states repeated each sentence word for word after the myth-teller who told the stories to me.

Our indigenous oral literatures can and should be made available, with suitable changes in content and style, to the Europeans who have entered and made their homes in the new continents. The richness as well as the variety of the literatures and cultural heritages of the American Indians can be introduced to children in such adapted stories as these, which are not as remote from the original as is usually the case in retellings of non-European folklores. Above all, anything which we can do to develop respect and affection in our children for the cultural, imaginative, and artistic heritages of other peoples, especially those having darker skin color or inferior technology and economy, is all to the good. Adults who wish to acquaint themselves with regional folklores should, however, read the original text translations, where the folklorist has not resorted to those changes that at present appear to be desirable for a youthful audience.

MELVILLE JACOBS
Associate Professor of Anthropology
University of Washington
Seattle